Mr Bear Babysits

Debi Gliori

ORCHARD BOOKS

for Leslie Gardiner

my dear friend

with lots of love

ORCHARD BOOKS
96 Leonard Street, London EC2A 4RH
Orchard Books Australia
14 Mars Road, Lane Cove, NSW 2066
ISBN 1 85213 629 4 (hardback)
ISBN 1 85213 843 2 (paperback)
First published in Great Britain 1994
First paperback publication 1995
Text and illustrations © Debi Gliori 1994
The right of Debi Gliori to be identified as the author and illustrator
of this work has been asserted by her in accordance with the
Copyright, Designs and Patents Act, 1988.
A CIP catalogue record for this book is available from the British Library.
Printed in Belgium

"It's no use," said Mrs Bear. "I can't seem to settle the baby."

"Mmm?" said Mr Bear.

"I can't take her with me to babysit for the Grizzle-
Bears," said Mrs Bear. "She'd keep them all awake."
"Mmm-hmm," said Mr Bear.
"So you'll have to babysit," said Mrs Bear.
"Mmm," said Mr Bear. "WHAT?"

Mr Bear walked through the woods to the Grizzle-Bears' house and knocked on the door. Before he could say "I've come to babysit," a baby bear was thrust into his arms.

"We're late, so late, so terribly late," said Mr and Mrs Grizzle-Bear as they bolted out of the door.

Mr Bear felt his arms becoming sticky.

"You'll have to give the baby a bath," said a small bear appearing at the end of the hall.

Mr Bear didn't know how to bath a baby. His wife had always taken care of that kind of thing.

"You're not very good at that," said Fred as Mr Bear drenched himself in bathwater.

"That's not the right way to do it," said Ted as Mr Bear tried to dry himself and the baby with the bath mat.

"I don't think you're a proper babysitter," said Fuzz as the baby started to cry.

Mr Bear didn't know how to stop babies from crying. He patted the baby's head and rocked the baby up and down.

"You're not very good at that," said Fred.

So Mr Bear tried to sing a lullaby.

> *"Twinkle, twinkle little slug,*
> *Leaving slime trails on the rug . . ."*

"That's not the right way to do it," said Ted.

"I really don't think you're a proper babysitter,"
said Fuzz. The baby went on crying.
"Perhaps the baby's hungry," said Mr Bear.
And he headed towards the kitchen.

Fred, Ted and Fuzz watched Mr Bear prepare a meal of raw fish. The baby wouldn't eat it.

"You're not very good at that," said Fred.

Then Mr Bear tried some acorn mush and the baby spat it out.

"Don't you know that babies only eat honey? I'm *sure* you're not a proper babysitter," said Fuzz.

So Mr Bear gave the baby some honey. The baby's eyes began to close.

"It really is very peaceful," sighed Mr Bear
as he settled down into a comfortable chair.
"I wonder what the others are doing?"

BONGA BONGA TWANGGG CRRRASHHH

The baby woke up and began to cry again.

"We were playing hide-and-seek," said Fred.
" ...but Fuzz hid in the clock," said Ted.
"...and it wobbled too far," said Fuzz.

"THAT'S IT!" shouted Mr Bear.

"You're quite good at shouting," said Fred.

"UPSTAIRS. BED. NOW!" roared Mr Bear.

"That's the right way to do it," said Ted.

"AND NOT A PEEP OUT OF ANY OF YOU, OR THERE WILL BE TROUBLE!" boomed Mr Bear.

"You *are* a proper babysitter after all," said Fuzz. And they ran off and dived into bed.

Mr Bear and the baby went back to the bathroom.
Mr Bear washed and brushed the baby brilliantly.
Mr Bear and the baby went into the kitchen.

Mr Bear cleaned up the mess, made himself a cup of tea, loaded a plate with biscuits and warmed a little honey, all the while humming a soothing lullaby to keep the baby happy.

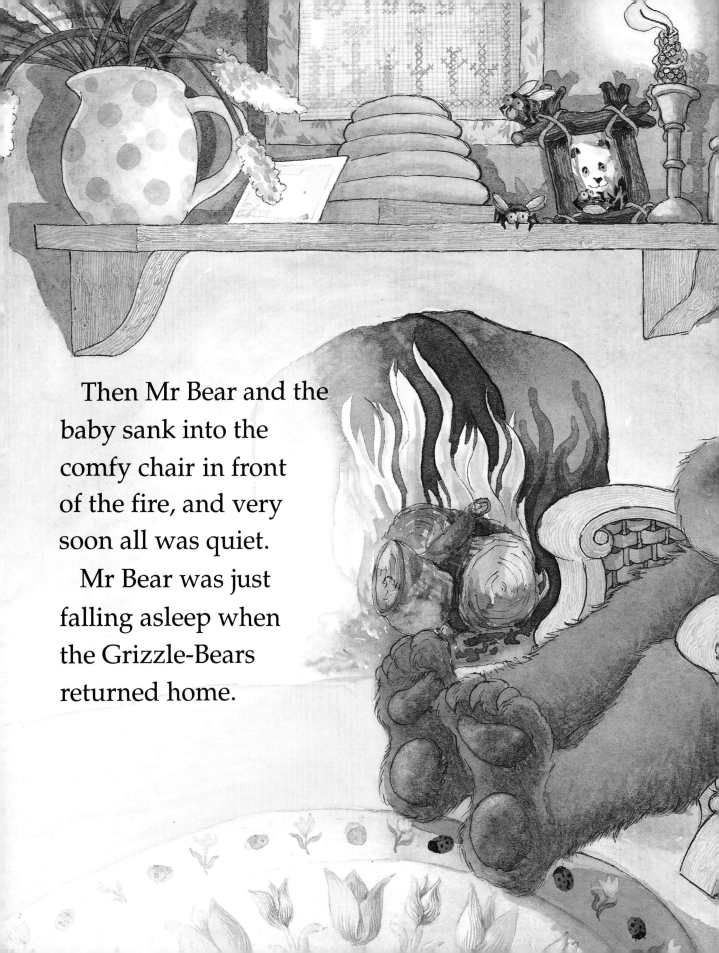

Then Mr Bear and the baby sank into the comfy chair in front of the fire, and very soon all was quiet.

Mr Bear was just falling asleep when the Grizzle-Bears returned home.

"Don't know *how* you got that baby to sleep," said
Mrs Grizzle-Bear. "I always let my husband take care of
that kind of thing."

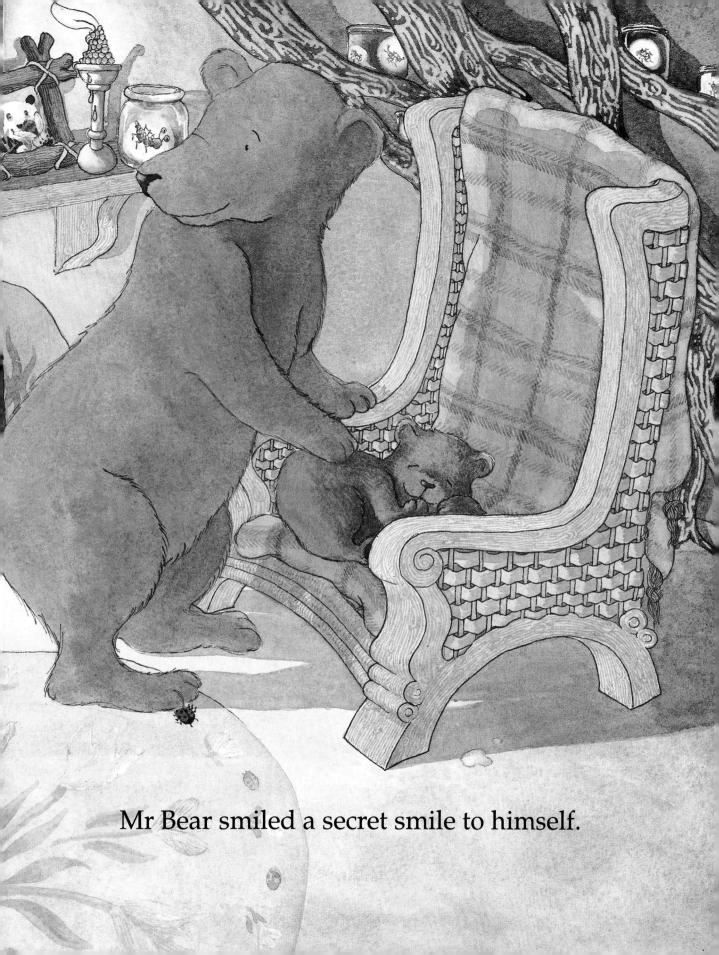

Mr Bear smiled a secret smile to himself.

Mr Bear walked home by moonlight past burrows and nests where babies and children were being tucked in and lights were turned low for the night.

Mr Bear's secret smile grew wider.

When he reached home, Mr Bear could hear his own baby *still* crying.

Mr Bear tiptoed inside.

"Can I help?" he said.
"Could you hold her for a
minute, while I make us both
a cup of blueberry tea?" said Mrs Bear.

So Mr Bear held their baby in his lap
and sang her a lullaby.

Her cries turned to little hiccupy sobs, and then to hiccups, and finally, with a small burp, she closed her eyes.

When Mrs Bear brought in the tea,
she found Mr Bear and their baby fast asleep.